D1442958

Dear Parents:

Congratulations! Your child is taking the first steps on an exciting journey. The destination? Independent reading!

STEP INTO READING® will help your child get there. The program offers five steps to reading success. Each step includes fun stories and colorful art or photographs. In addition to original fiction and books with favorite characters, there are Step into Reading Non-Fiction Readers, Phonics Readers and Boxed Sets, Sticker Readers, and Comic Readers—a complete literacy program with something to interest every child.

Learning to Read, Step by Step!

Ready to Read   Preschool–Kindergarten
• big type and easy words • rhyme and rhythm • picture clues
For children who know the alphabet and are eager to begin reading.

Reading with Help   Preschool–Grade 1
• basic vocabulary • short sentences • simple stories
For children who recognize familiar words and sound out new words with help.

Reading on Your Own   Grades 1–3
• engaging characters • easy-to-follow plots • popular topics
For children who are ready to read on their own.

Reading Paragraphs   Grades 2–3
• challenging vocabulary • short paragraphs • exciting stories
For newly independent readers who read simple sentences with confidence.

Ready for Chapters   Grades 2–4
• chapters • longer paragraphs • full-color art
For children who want to take the plunge into chapter books but still like colorful pictures.

STEP INTO READING® is designed to give every child a successful reading experience. The grade levels are only guides; children will progress through the steps at their own speed, developing confidence in their reading. The F&P Text Level on the back cover serves as another tool to help you choose the right book for your child.

Remember, a lifetime love of reading starts with a single step!

For Griffin—may you always fly home!
—M.L.

To Elizabeth Morris
—H.W.

Text copyright © 2007 by Mallory Loehr
Illustrations copyright © 2007 by Hala Wittwer

Visit us on the Web!
StepIntoReading.com
randomhousekids.com

Educators and librarians, for a variety of teaching tools, visit us at
RHTeachersLibrarians.com

Library of Congress Cataloging-in-Publication Data
Loehr, Mallory.
Dragon egg / by Mallory Loehr ; illustrated by Hala Wittwer.
    p.   cm. — (Step into reading. Step 1)
Summary: A dragon's egg rolls out of its nest in a cave, continuing along a road,
past a castle, and through a town, where it bumps against a rock and cracks.
ISBN: 978-0-375-84350-1 (trade) — ISBN: 978-0-375-94350-8 (lib. bdg.)
[1. Eggs—Fiction. 2. Dragons—Fiction.] I. Wittwer, Hala, ill. II. Title.
PZ7.L82615Dr 2007
[E]—dc22   2006027015

Printed in the United States of America   30 29 28 27 26 25 24 23 22 21 20

This book has been officially leveled by using the F&P Text Level Gradient™ Leveling System.

Dragon Egg

by Mallory Loehr
illustrated by Hala Wittwer

Random House 🏠 New York

Dragon eggs in a nest.

Dragon mama takes
a rest.

One egg tips.

Then it rolls.

The egg rolls
out of the nest!

The egg rolls
out of the cave.

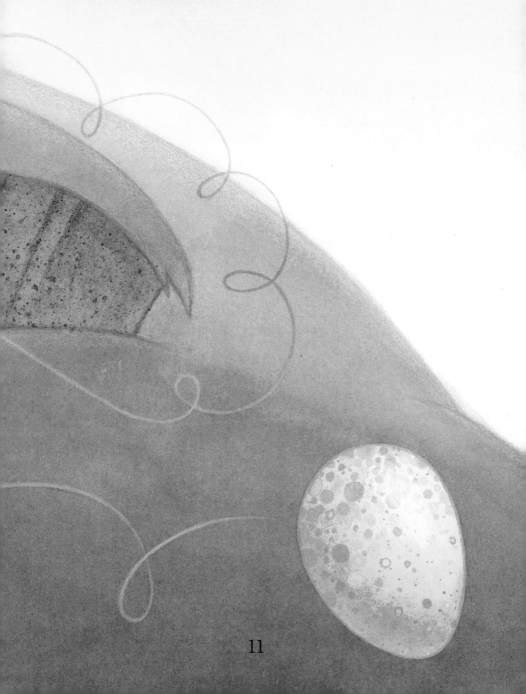

The egg rolls
down the hill.

The egg rolls
along the road.

The egg rolls

past a castle.

The egg rolls

through a town.

The egg rolls
off a cliff.

BANG!

The egg cracks open!

The baby dragon opens
his mouth. . . .

Pfff!

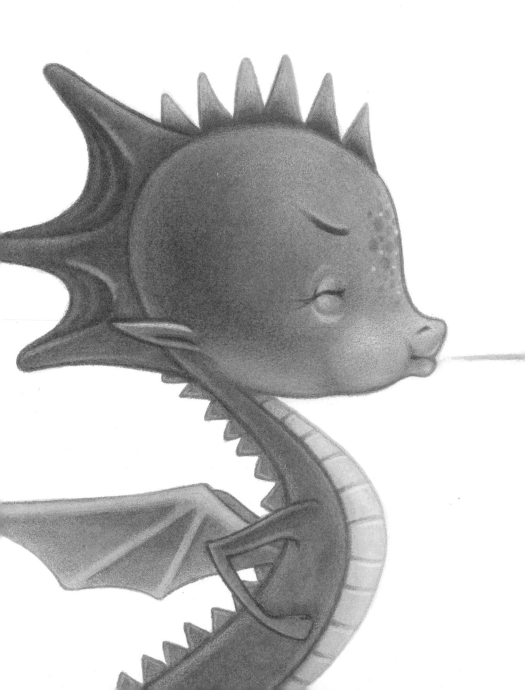

Out comes a little fire!

The baby dragon flies
through the town.

The baby dragon flies
past the castle.

The baby dragon flies
along the road.

The baby dragon flies
up the hill.

The baby dragon flies
into the cave.

Look who is waiting!